The Harrie Taylor Mysteries

Kristine Fitzgerald

With illustrations by
Sienna Ham

Book One

The Missing Bracelet

Chapter 1

"Harriet Grace Taylor! Come here at once!"

Harrie quickly washed her face, splashed water through her hair and combed it into place. A few little bits poked out at strange angles but she pushed herself out of the bathroom and headed down the hall.

"There you are," her mother said, exasperated. "Hurry up and have some breakfast. We need to leave in half an hour."

"Leave?" Harrie said. "What do you mean *leave?*"

"I mean, we're leaving soon to go to the Jones' for their barbecue. You know, their Australia Day barbecue, the one we go to every year."

"Oh no, Mum. Don't make me go. Please. I can't stand Ella. She's so… prissy. And her little brother Ted—he's a spoilt brat."

"Don't speak like that. You're coming and that's final. You tell her, Ross."

Harrie's father looked up from his newspaper. "Tell her what?"

"Honestly," Harrie's mum exhaled, "you haven't heard a word that's been said, have you?"

Harrie's father pushed his glasses up until they sat above his forehead. "What's all this?"

"Tell her she's coming out for lunch today."

"Please Dad," Harrie begged. "Don't make me go."

He looked from Harrie to her mum then back again. The look that he saw on his wife's face made his decision very easy to make. "Of course you're coming with us, Harrie. You can't stay here on your own—you're too young."

"What if… what if Ben came over? Yes, Ben could come here, then I wouldn't be on my own."

Her mum stood up and took the orange juice out of the fridge. "Absolutely not. You're coming with us and that's all there is to it."

Harrie folded her arms in a huff. "Well then, Ben can come with us, can't he? Please Mum. Please Dad."

Harrie's father looked at his wife and once again he could read everything he needed to know from her expression. "Yes, that's fine. Ben can come. Call him straight away, then hurry up and have something to eat. We're leaving very soon."

Although Harrie still didn't want to go to the barbecue, it was going to be much better now that her best friend Ben was coming too. In fact, Ben was her only friend. Who else wanted to be friends with a girl in a wheelchair? Harrie couldn't run around like all the other children at school but Ben didn't mind.

They'd been friends for a long time now. Ben was very clever—he knew lots of trivia and he loved learning new facts. When he'd come over to Harrie's place two days ago, he'd told her all about echidnas and how their name comes from 'The Mother of Monsters' in ancient Greek mythology. Harrie found it hard to believe at first because echidnas were so cute and harmless but she knew better than to doubt anything that Ben said.

Harrie's father wheeled her out the front door while her mum picked up her bag and the pavlova that she had made.

"Hey, Mum. You're wearing your new bracelet."

"I am indeed. It's beautiful, isn't it? Your father spoils me. I love the way the diamonds catch the sunlight."

When they pulled up at Ben's house Harrie saw him waiting out the front. She waved to him through the window. Ben walked around to the driver's side of the car, climbed in and slammed the door behind him.

"Hi Ben," Harrie grinned. "How are you going?"

"Good thanks. Hi Mr and Mrs Taylor."

"Good morning Ben," Harrie's mum replied. "Put your seatbelt on and we'll be on our way. Did you bring your swimmers? There's a pool there."

"No, I'll be fine. I'll just hang out with Harrie."

Harrie was so glad to have Ben as her friend. Even when other people gave her a hard time and forgot that she wasn't able to do certain things, Ben understood. He just *got* it.

He turned to look at her. "Last night I was reading, right, and I read some stuff about earthquakes. Did you know that there are roughly half a million earthquakes every year?"

"In Australia?" Harrie asked.

"No, in the whole world. And most of them you can't even feel. So, you can be sitting there watching tv and there could be an earthquake at any time."

"But if we can't feel them, then it doesn't really matter, does it?"

"Of course it matters. They weaken the earth's crust so if there's another one in the same spot it would be a lot worse."

"Oh Ben," Harrie's mum said, "I'm sure it's not as bad as all that. Don't frighten Harrie."

Harrie sat up straight. "I'm not *scared*, Mum. Ben can talk about earthquakes if he wants to."

Her dad spoke up. "Well, we've arrived, so this conversation can be put on hold until later. Stay there Harrie and I'll get your chair."

Harrie smiled to herself. Her father told her to stay there but she could hardly go anywhere, could she?

They made their way up to the front door and Harrie's mother rang the doorbell.

"Come in, come in," Mrs Jones said as she opened the door. Don't you look lovely, Susan. Your bracelet is just divine. Is it new?"

"It is," Harrie's mother replied. "Ross gave it to me for my birthday."

"Aren't you a lucky thing? I wish Bob would give me romantic gifts like that. Anyway, come in, Come through the house—it's probably easier that way. We're all sitting out the back."

As Harrie was pushed through the living room and the kitchen, she saw three-year-old Ted waddling around on his chubby legs. "What's that Ted's got in his hand?"

"I'm not sure," Ben replied.

"Oh Ted!" Mrs Jones said in a loud voice. "You're a naughty boy. Give me those tongs back. Your father needs them for the barbecue."

Harrie's mother placed her handbag on one of the chairs in the dining room. "Ted's looking as gorgeous as always."

"Gorgeous?" Mrs Jones said. "He's a rascal, that one. He's always picking things up and putting them down somewhere else. Yesterday afternoon I couldn't find my car keys anywhere. I knew I'd left them on the table between the armchairs in the tv room but when I went to get them they weren't there. Fifteen minutes later I found them on the floor in the bathroom. I was running late then for the rest of the day."

"But how did you know it was Ted who took them?" Ben asked.

"Oh, I have no doubt that it was Ted. Ella was over at her friend's place and Bob was outside mowing the lawns. It was Ted, all right. He's a little monkey."

Chapter 2

Mrs Jones opened the back door so that Harrie's dad could wheel Harrie through easily. "Most people have arrived already. You know the Cormacks and the Whites. And there's my mum over near the pool with Ella. She's been here for a few days and is spoiling the kids rotten."

Harrie settled herself under the shade of a tree and Ben dragged a chair over so that he could sit down too. "There's no-one our age here," Harrie said. "They're all little kids."

Ben looked around. "Yeah, I see what you mean. Who's that little girl in the fancy dress?"

"That's Ella. She lives here and she's the biggest pain. Look at her twirling around and showing off."

Harrie and Ben watched as Ella danced in front of her grandmother. She was dressed in a blue puffy dress, high heels and she wore a tiara on her head.

"She's even got a fake necklace and earrings on," Ben commented.

"Yep," Harrie sighed. "That's Ella for you. She loves being the centre of attention."

Harrie didn't wear any jewellery and she kept her hair cut short. She owned one dress for special occasions but that was only because her mother said she had to. Harrie had never worn it—not even once. She wore shorts and t-shirts in the summer and a jumper and jeans in the winter, or if she was staying at home she'd put tracksuit pants on because they were so warm and comfortable.

As they looked on, Harrie and Ben saw Ella take her grandmother's hand and drag her towards the house. "Come with me, Nana. I want to show you my dolly. Her name's Melissa and she's in my bedroom."

Ella's grandmother followed obediently. "All right, all right, I'm coming. Look, don't leave your cup behind. I'll take it into the kitchen with us. Ella, wait. You've left your little handbag on the grass. Hold on a minute and I'll take it in as well."

Ella's grandmother smiled at Harrie and Ben and gave them a wink as she walked past. "I'll sleep well tonight, having looked after this one all day. It's exhausting!"

Harrie leaned over and giggled as she whispered into Ben's ear. "She's got a lot of perfume on, hasn't she?"

"I'll say," Ben agreed.

"She smells like roses and vanilla. Yuk."

"Is that what it is?"

"That's what I think. Roses on their own would be OK and vanilla on its own would actually be really nice, but together it's too strong. Thank goodness we're outside, otherwise we'd be breathing it in all day."

Ben laughed. That was one thing he really like about Harrie—she always said exactly what she was thinking. Some people only said things that were nice but that meant they weren't necessarily telling the truth. Harrie always told the truth and she didn't care who was listening.

Her dad walked over towards them. "I'm about to get drinks. What can I get for you two?"

"What did we bring?" Harrie asked.

"Lemonade and apple juice. What would you prefer, Harrie?"

"Apple juice please."

"And you, Ben? What can I get you to drink?"

"I'll have a lemonade please, Mr Taylor."

"Coming right up. I won't be long."

Ben reached down and took his shoes and socks off. "Gee, it's hot, isn't it?"

"It sure is," Harrie answered. "My t-shirt is sticking to my back. But it's better than being at school. We start back next week."

"Yes, we do. I don't mind going back. In fact I'm looking forward to it, but only if I get Mr Corey. He's a really good teacher. He's actually been to Egypt and studied the pyramids."

"Has he?" Harrie said vaguely. "School's OK, I suppose. But I'd rather stay home and watch a good movie any day."

"Or read," Ben quickly added. "You're such a bookworm. Have you finished the Sherlock Holmes series yet?"

"I sure have. I was given the two latest books for Christmas and I'd finished them both before New Year."

Harrie's Dad returned and handed them their drinks. "I'm going to go and help Bob cook the sausages. Your mother's just over there talking to the Whites. You two are OK here, aren't you?"

"Of course we are, Dad," Harrie said as she rolled her eyes. "It's not like we're three years old."

"Good. Just let me know if you need anything."

Chapter 3

Mrs Jones walked up to Harrie and Ben carrying a bowl of chips in one hand and a bowl of nuts in the other. "Would you like something to eat?" she asked. "Help yourself."

They both picked up a handful of chips and mumbled "Thank you."

"And how are you, Harrie?" Mrs Jones asked. "Have you enjoyed the summer?"

"It's been OK, I guess."

"Bob and I took our two children to Water World last week and they had a ball. What have you been doing? Lots of fun things, I hope."

"Not much. Mostly staying at home."

"Surely you've done more than that, dear. It's been such a beautiful summer this year."

Harrie tried to think what she could say. "Mum and I had lunch the other day at Rascals. That was pretty good, I guess."

"Yes, that sounds lovely. Have a few more chips, both of you, before I go. I need to get around everyone because lunch will be ready soon."

Harrie munched on her chips and looked at Ben. She noticed he had a scowl on his face. "What's up?"

"That woman who was just here. She's a piece of work, don't you think?"

"Mrs Jones? She's all right. What makes you say that?"

"She was awful. She didn't speak to me once—it was like I wasn't even there. And asking you whether you've done any fun stuff like going to water parks. She should know you can't do things like that."

"I guess," Harrie said. "I don't think she meant anything by it though."

"And she's just so… I don't know… so posh."

Harrie giggled. "You make me laugh sometimes, Ben. Don't worry about her though. There are plenty of worse people than her."

They watched as Mrs Jones offered the snacks to an older couple who were sitting nearby.

"That's a gorgeous hat Eileen," they overheard Mrs Jones say. "I just love it."

"This? It's been in the cupboard for years. I had to dust it off before I put it on today."

"Nonsense. I don't believe that for a minute. It looks brand new."

Ben leaned in close to Harrie. "That's another thing. She's always admiring other people's clothes and things. She was all over your mum's bracelet when we arrived here."

"She's just being nice."

"It's not nice when she sounds so fake."

"Whatever," Harrie shrugged. "Let's talk about something else."

Suddenly there was the sound of a child crying. Harrie looked up and saw Ted coming down the yard, this time carrying a plastic toy. He was hurrying towards his mother with a snotty nose and tears running down his cheeks.

Mrs Jones turned around, placed the bowls of chips and nuts on the table and held her arms out to him. "Come here, my baby boy. What's the matter?" She scooped him up but he continued to cry. "My, my, you're tired, aren't you? I'll have to put you to bed soon for a little nap."

Harrie's mum walked up to Mrs Jones. "Can I help at all? Is there anything I can do?"

"I don't think so. I'm just trying to settle Ted here. Could you get this Buzz Lightyear toy out of his hand for me?"

Harrie's mother tried to prise the toy from Ted but he held on firmly. "No," he called in a sharp voice.

Harrie and Ben looked at each other. "I didn't even know he could speak," Harrie said.

"Don't worry about it thanks, Susan. Buzz is one of his favourites at the moment. I'll get it from him in a minute. Would you mind passing around these bowls? I'm sure lunch will be ready soon."

"No problem at all."

Harrie's mum picked up the bowls and offered them to the remaining guests while Ted wriggled his way out of his mother's arms.

"Don't you go far, young man. And don't get up to any mischief!"

Just then Harrie heard the back door of the house slam shut. She looked up and saw Ella coming out with her grandmother. Ella was marching down the backyard holding a doll wrapped in a flannelette blanket. "Hurry up Nana," the little girl said. "We're going to do Melissa's hair."

The older lady followed Ella and the two of them found a couple of chairs in the shade not far from the pool. "No, not like that," Ella demanded. "Give me the brush. I know how to do it properly."

"Ugh," Harrie said quietly. "I'm glad I don't have a little sister."

"Speak for yourself," Ben said. "You can have my sister if you like."

"No thanks. At least your sister's not into dolls and everything though. She's OK."

"Some days she is. Other days she's a nightmare. She ran into me on her scooter last week. I've still got a bruise on my leg."

"All right everybody," Mr Jones called in a loud voice. "Lunch is ready. Come and help yourselves."

Ben stood up. "I'll go and get you something. What would you like?"

"A sausage sandwich please," Harrie replied.

"Sauce?"

"Yes and mustard too, if they have it."

"OK, I'll be back in a sec."

Ben returned a few minutes later with Harrie's sandwich and a burger for himself. "They have salad too, if you want. I didn't get any though because I already had enough stuff to carry."

"That's OK. Thanks Ben." Harrie placed her plate on her lap and started to eat.

"Yum. This burger's pretty good," Ben said.

"What's on it?"

"The meat patty, a cheese slice and tomato and barbecue sauce."

"*Both* sauces?"

"Yeah, why not?"

"That's disgusting."

"No, it's not. You should try it. It's the best."

"I'll take your word for it."

While Harrie was eating she saw her dad come up to her. "You two have some food already? That's good to see. What about drinks? Can I get you anything?"

"No, I'm fine thanks Dad."

"And you, Ben? Would you like some more lemonade?"

"Yes please. If that's OK. I can get it myself if you like."

"No, stay there and keep eating your lunch. I'll be right back."

Two minutes later Harrie's dad made his way back, carrying Ben's drink and a plate of food. Rather than coming through the crowd of people he walked along the path beside the pool.

"Ross!" a loud voice called. "Where are you going? Come and sit over here with us!"

Harrie looked across and saw Mr Jones waving his arms, indicating that her dad should go and sit with him.

"I'm coming," he replied. "Hold on a second. I'm just taking this drink to Ben."

In the short amount of time that had passed, Harrie's dad's concentration had been interrupted and he wasn't looking where he was going. Before he knew it he tripped over something on the ground in front of him.

"Oh no," Harrie gasped as she raised her hands up to her mouth. She watched as her father fell to the ground. Ben's lemonade landed on the path—luckily it was in a plastic cup—but her dad's lunch flew through the air and landed in the swimming pool.

Chapter 4

"Quick Ben, wheel me over there. I need to see if Dad's OK."

Harrie's father pushed himself up to a sitting position and rubbed his elbow.

"Are you all right, Dad? Let me have a look at you."

"I'm fine, Harrie. I banged my elbow a bit but it's OK."

"No, it's not OK. You're bleeding. Quick Ben, grab me a few serviettes, will you?"

By this time more people had hurried over, including Harrie's mum. She sat down on the side of the pool and picked up the loose bits of bread, lettuce, cheese and tomato that were floating on the surface. She reached down into the water to pick up the piece of steak that had sunk and landed on the top step.

"Yuk," she said as she placed the soggy food on the paper plate. "You've made a mess of this, Ross. Are you sure you're all right?"

"Yes, I'm OK. You can all stop fussing." He stood up. "Look. I'm fine, see? Just a little scratch but nothing serious. Let's all go back and enjoy our lunch."

Ben wheeled Harrie back to their shady spot and they watched as Mr and Mrs Jones talked to Harrie's parents. "There's plenty more food Ross," Mr Jones said. 'Help yourself to some more."

"I will, thanks. I'll throw another steak sandwich together and be with you before long."

Once the leftovers had all been cleared away, Mrs Jones started to bring out some desserts. Harrie's mum stood up quickly and walked past Harrie and Ben as she headed towards the house.

"Mum!" Harrie called.

"Not now, Harrie. I need to get the pav out of the fridge."

"But Mum, wait!"

"What is it?"

"Your bracelet. Where's your bracelet?"

"It's right here," Harrie's mother replied. But as she looked down at her wrist, she could see that her bracelet was missing.

"That's right, I remember now. I took it off so I could reach into the pool to pick up the food that your father dropped. It's OK. I'll get it right away."

Harrie frowned. Her mother's bracelet was very expensive and shouldn't be left lying around in someone else's backyard. "Where did you leave it?"

Harrie's mum pointed. "On that chair there, right beside the pool."

"Down near the deep end?"

"Yes, I placed it there on my way to where your father had fallen. I need to go, Harrie. I need to get the bracelet and bring the pav out."

Harrie looked on closely as her mother approached the chair where she had left her bracelet. She watched in dismay as her mum looked around the chair, under the chair and on the ground near the chair.

"I knew it!" Harrie muttered. "The bracelet's not there. Quick Ben, wheel me over to Mum. We need to help her find her bracelet."

Ben jumped up, quickly moved a few obstacles out of the way and pushed Harrie along the path beside the pool.

"It's… it's not here," Harrie's mum said when they arrived. "My bracelet… it's missing!"

"Look on the grass, Mum. Just in case someone knocked it off accidentally."

"I have. I've looked everywhere. My bracelet's gone!"

Harrie noticed the tears that were forming in her mother's eyes. "It's all right, Mum. We'll find it but you should probably tell Dad what's going on."

"Yes, you're right."

Harrie's mum looked at Ben. "Be a love, would you Ben, and bring the pavlova outside for me? It's in the fridge in the kitchen."

Harrie's patience quickly disappeared. "Don't worry about the stupid dessert, Mum! You've lost your bracelet. That's way more important."

"Yes, yes, you're right. Oh dear. How could I have let this happen?" She pulled a handkerchief out of her pocket and dabbed at her eyes as she walked off to find her husband.

Harrie's parents returned very quickly. Her father looked around but he, too, couldn't find anything. "Tell me what happened again," he said.

"Like I just said, when you fell over I hurried to see if you were all right. I was near the back door of the house, so I took my bracelet off while I was walking and I put it on this chair. Right here. But now it's gone and I don't know where it is."

Harrie's father shook his head. "Someone must know where it's gone. It can't just vanish into thin air. I'm going to call everyone over."

"No, Ross. Surely there's no need for that."

"Yes, there is. We need to find your bracelet."

Harrie's father walked back to where everyone was sitting. "Excuse me everybody," he called in a loud voice. "Could I have your attention for a moment?"

All the adults stopped talking and turned around to face Harrie's dad. "Sorry to interrupt but I need your help."

Mr Jones stood up and walked towards Harrie's dad. He could tell that whatever had happened was quite serious.

"Just before lunch," Harrie's dad continued, "Susan removed her jewellery. She left it on that chair over there but now it's gone missing. Has anyone seen it?"

"Seen what exactly?" Mr Jones asked.

"A bracelet. It's a diamond bracelet."

A few seconds passed and no-one said anything. "Right then," Mr Jones boomed, "we need to look for it. Everybody up out of your seats, please. I'm sure with you all helping we'll find the bracelet in no time."

Just as everyone was standing up and starting to look, Mrs Jones came out of the house carrying a chocolate cake. "What's going on?" she asked. "What are you all doing?"

Mr Jones took the cake from her and placed it on the table. "Susan has lost her bracelet. She took it off and left it on that chair."

"Why would she do that?"

"It was when Ross fell over. She took it off so she could help clean up. Don't you remember? She picked up all the loose bits of food out of the pool."

"I see. Well, dessert will have to wait. I'll have a quick look inside."

"It's not inside. She knows where she left it."

"Yes, but it's not there. It could be anywhere, Bob. It won't hurt to have a quick look."

"I guess so. I'll stay out here. I think it's much more likely to be somewhere in the yard."

Chapter 5

Fifteen minutes or more passed and the bracelet hadn't been found. Harrie's dad called out to everyone once more. "Thank you everybody. I think we've done all we can for now. Thanks for your help."

Mrs Jones put her arm around Harrie's mum's shoulders. "Try not to worry, Susan. Your bracelet *must* be here somewhere. As soon as it turns up, I'll call you and let you know."

"Thank you," Harrie's mum said with tears in her eyes. "I really want it back."

"Of course you do. It's a beautiful bracelet."

The mood of the barbecue had changed now—it was no longer a relaxed, lazy summer afternoon—so people started to pack up and head home.

Ben leaned over and whispered in Harrie's ear. "You don't think anyone has *stolen* the bracelet, do you?"

"I don't know, Ben. It's possible. But now that people are leaving, if someone *has* taken it, we may never see it again."

"Well, it sounds like another case for you to solve, Harrie. This is what you're good at. The adults have done all they can, so it's up to you to solve the mystery of what happened to your mum's bracelet."

Harrie's face lit up. "That's just what I was thinking. I'll need your help, Ben. We'll have to look for clues, interview suspects…"

Harrie's train of thought was interrupted when her mum walked over.

"Come on, you two. We're getting our things together and going home."

"No!" Harrie said quickly. "We can't leave yet. We haven't got your bracelet."

"We've looked everywhere and haven't been able to find it. Come on now, it's time to go."

"I just need a few minutes, Mum. Let me look for some clues, at least."

"You have five minutes and that's all. As soon as your father and I have put everything in the car we're going home."

"That's OK. Five minutes will do." She turned to Ben. "We need to get to work. Can you push me over to where Dad fell?"

Ben released the handbrake on Harrie's wheelchair and pushed her to the side of the pool. She couldn't see anything on the path but in the grass nearby she found one of Ted's toys. "Look," she said to Ben excitedly. "See that toy over there? It might be a clue. Can you pick it up?"

Ben fetched the toy from the grass. "It's Buzz Lightyear," he said as he handed it to Harrie. "It definitely belongs to Ted. We saw him holding it earlier."

"Right," Harrie said. She was thinking quickly because she knew she didn't have much time. "Have you got your notebook?"

"Of course I have. You know I always carry it with me."
Ben pulled a small notebook and pencil out from the back
pocket of his shorts.

"Good. Write down Buzz Lightyear. Found on the grass
near where Dad fell. We can think more about it later."

"Got it," Ben replied. "What next?"

Harrie looked around. "There's nothing else here. Dad's
lunch fell into the pool and his plate landed on the path but
Mum cleaned all that up. Push me down to the deep end,
can you?"

"Sure. Why do you need to go there?"

"Because that's where Mum took her bracelet off."

They moved to the other end of the pool and had one
more good look around the chair.

"I still can't believe Mum just took her bracelet off and
left it sitting here."

"She probably wasn't thinking clearly," Ben said.

"I suppose so. But it's her bracelet! She should have come back for it."

"We don't have very long," Ben reminded Harrie. "Let's just look for clues."

"You're right but there's nothing here."

"Just a bit of rubbish," Ben added.

"Do you think that could mean anything?"

"Probably not but we should still check it out."

"OK, pick up that tissue then, would you?"

"Yuk. I don't want to pick up someone's dirty tissue!"

"Ben," Harrie insisted, "it was your idea. Just pick it up and put it in your pocket."

"No way. I'm going to get a plastic bag." He ran off and returned with a small Ziplock bag.

"Good," Harrie said. "Pick it up and keep it. Quick, here comes Mum. We're going to have to go now."

Ben reluctantly picked the tissue up from the ground, put it in the bag, then stuffed it into his pocket. He wiped his hands on his shorts and made a quick note that the tissue had been collected from underneath the chair where the bracelet had been left.

Harrie looked around once more. "I can't see anything else. I think that's all we're going to get."

Chapter 6

Later that afternoon Harrie and Ben were getting hungry again so they decided to have a snack.

"What do you feel like?" Harrie asked.

"Have you got any muesli bars?"

"We should have. Let me check in the pantry."

Harrie pushed herself to the tall cupboard in the corner of the kitchen and opened the door. Everything that she was likely to need was kept at a height she could reach. She moved a few boxes of cereal to the side but was unable to find any muesli bars.

"No, we're out. I'll have to let Mum know so she can get some more."

"What *have* you got then?"

Harrie continued to look. "There's Pizza Shapes and Tiny Teddies. That's about all. Otherwise there are apples and bananas in the fruit bowl."

"How about we make banana smoothies?" Ben suggested. "I'll have a look to see how much milk you've got in the fridge."

Harrie reversed her wheelchair out of the pantry and followed Ben. He held up a bottle of milk that was half full. "This should do, shouldn't it?"

"Yes, that will be enough. I'll let Mum know we're also getting low on milk. The blender's in that cupboard. Can you get it out?"

Ben squatted down to the floor, opened the cupboard and pulled out the blender. He plugged it in and gathered together the ingredients that were needed. "I've got milk and bananas. That's all we need, isn't it?"

"You haven't made smoothies before, have you?" Harrie said in a very matter of fact tone. "We need something to sweeten it. Sometimes I just use maple syrup but ice cream's heaps better. Can you get the ice cream out of the freezer?"

Harrie chopped up the bananas, Ben scooped the ice cream and they put it all together in the blender along with the milk. "Now hold the lid on tight," Harrie instructed. She pressed the button and the blender started to whir. "You can pour it, Ben. It's a bit full for me to manage. Fill both glasses right up."

Ben carried the smoothies to the table and they drank them quickly.

"That was really good," Ben said. "I might make smoothies at home. It was just banana and ice cream, wasn't it?"

"And milk."

"Yeah, of course. Speaking of milk, did you know that cows have a really good sense of smell? They can smell things that are up to ten kilometres away."

"No way!" Harrie said. "That's from here to the other side of town."

"It's true," Ben said. "And in the olden days, before people had fridges, they used to keep milk in buckets. And to make sure the milk didn't go off they threw one or two frogs into the bucket with it."

Harrie studied Ben's face to make sure he wasn't joking but his expression remained serious. "You've got to be kidding."

"I'm not," Ben said simply. "The frogs have some sort of antibiotic on their skin that keeps the milk fresh."

"That's so disgusting. I'm glad I'm alive now and not back then. Anyway, we need to get back to the case."

"Yeah, your mum's bracelet. Do you have any idea who might have taken it?"

"We can't go making assumptions," Harrie said sternly. "We don't know if it's stolen, we only know that it's missing. So, let's stick to the facts."

"OK," Ben said shyly. Sometimes he thought that Harrie spoke a bit harshly and he assumed it was because she had more challenging things to face than most other kids did. "What are the facts so far?"

"We gathered the clues before we left. We've got Buzz Lightyear and a dirty tissue."

"That doesn't sound like much to go on."

"Maybe. Maybe not. Let's work through them together. Can you get the tissue out?"

Ben dug the plastic bag out of his pocket and placed it on the table in front of Harrie. "I'm not touching it again," he said.

"Don't be ridiculous. It's just a tissue and it might help us figure out what happened." She picked the tissue up and looked at it from different angles. "I can't see anything unusual."

Harrie then held the tissue up near her nose and had a quick sniff.

"Ben!" she said. "Smell this!"

"No thanks," Ben replied as he stepped back.

"I mean it. You have to smell it and tell me what you think!"

Ben reluctantly stepped forward and smelt the tissue. His eyes rose up to meet Harrie's as he realised he recognised the smell. "I've smelt this before."

"Yes, we both have," Harrie explained. "Roses and vanilla. It smells like Ella and Ted's grandmother's perfume. It must have been her tissue!"

"But does that mean anything?" Ben asked.

"It might. It places her at the scene, so we have to keep that in mind."

"Do you think Ted and Ella's grandmother might have taken the bracelet?"

"Yes, I do. We've got to consider the possibility."

"But she seemed so nice. I can't imagine her being a thief."

"Ben, we've known each other long enough that you should know by now not to jump to conclusions. We just have to gather the clues and work our way through them. But yes, their grandmother is now a suspect."

"What other suspects do we have?"

"It's possible that Ted picked it up. Maybe he thought it was a toy or something. We found Buzz Lightyear and that's our only other clue."

Harrie and Ben both thought for a few moments about who else might have taken the bracelet.

"Any of the women could have taken it," Harrie said. "It's a beautiful bracelet."

"Or any of the men could have picked it up to give to their wives."

"That's true."

"I just had another idea!" Ben said. "I know who might have taken it. It could have been Mrs Jones."

"What makes you say that?"

"Just the way she is. She seemed kind of fake and dressed really nicely like she wanted to impress everyone."

Harrie frowned. She didn't think this was a good enough reason to make Mrs Jones a suspect.

"And do you remember when we arrived? She said to your mum, 'Your bracelet is just divine' and 'I wish Bob would give me romantic gifts like that'."

"She did say those things," Harrie admitted. "But that doesn't mean she *took* it."

"It might," Ben said. "We've got to consider the possibility, haven't we?"

"OK, I guess so," Harrie reluctantly agreed. "So, we've got three suspects: Ted, his mum and his grandmother. At least we've made a start."

Chapter 7

"Mum," Harrie said at breakfast the next day. "Can we go around to the Jones' this morning? We need to find your bracelet."

"No, Harrie. We looked everywhere yesterday. And they would have rung me if it had turned up."

"But Mum," Harrie insisted, "you can't just give up. We need to keep trying."

"Well, I *was* planning to go over there sometime soon."

"See!" Harrie said. "Can't we go this morning? Please Mum?"

"I don't see why not. I don't have anything on today until later."

"Great! Thanks Mum." Harrie pushed her chair away from the table to go and get ready.

"Just a minute, Harrie. Come back here and finish your cereal."

"I'm full." But when Harrie's mum gave her 'the look' Harrie returned to the table and shoveled a few more spoonfuls into her mouth before leaving the room.

They picked Ben up on the way and drove to the next suburb where the Jones family lived. Mrs Jones invited them inside and offered them a cool drink.

"Did you manage to get some sleep last night?" Mrs Jones asked, looking directly at Harrie's mum.

"Not much."

"Me either. I feel so awful that you lost such a beautiful piece of jewellery while you were here."

Ben shot Harrie a sharp look. She knew what he was thinking: he was convinced that Mrs Jones had stolen the bracelet but Harrie was determined to keep an open mind.

"Do you mind if we ask you a few questions?" Harrie said as Mrs Jones placed a glass of cordial on the table in front of her.

"Of course not. What would you like to know?"

"I was wondering if perhaps Ted might have picked up the bracelet by mistake. You said yesterday that he's always picking things up, so I wondered where he might have put it, if he picked it up by accident."

Harrie worried that Mrs Jones might think she was trying to *blame* Ted. That wasn't the case at all—she just wanted to find out what had happened. But to her relief Mrs Jones laughed.

"You make a good point there," she said. "That's just the type of thing he would do. But I'm afraid if he did pick up the bracelet he could have dropped it anywhere."

"I see," Harrie said. She wasn't getting very far at all. "At least it would still be in this house, I suppose. We would just have to find out where."

Harrie's mum spoke up. "Now, now, we don't know that Ted took the bracelet. Anything could have happened to it. And anyway, didn't Ted have a nap around that time?"

Harrie sat bolt upright. Ted had a nap! Why hadn't she thought of that? She turned to face Mrs Jones again. "*When* did Ted have his nap exactly?"

"I don't remember *exactly*," Mrs Jones replied. "He usually has one in the late morning."

Ben tapped Harrie on the shoulder. "Didn't Ted come over near us before lunch? Don't you remember?" He looked at Mrs Jones. "It was when you were offering us the chips."

Mrs Jones nodded. "That's right, I think."

"Yes!" Harrie said. "He had Buzz Lightyear in his hand."

"He did," said Mrs Jones. "I was going to take him inside straight away. That's when you took over handing the chips around, Susan."

"But he can't have gone straight to bed because we found Buzz Lightyear on the ground later."

"That's right. I put him down, refilled the drinks for the Whites and the Cormacks and then I took him inside for his nap. It was only a few minutes later."

Harrie frowned. "So, he couldn't possibly have picked up the bracelet because he was already in bed, well before Dad tripped over. Did he have a long nap?"

"Oh yes, he didn't wake until after everyone had left. It was nearly three o'clock."

"It definitely wasn't Ted," Ben stated. Harrie knew he was right.

Just then Ella ran into the room with her grandmother following close behind.

"What are you up to, young lady?" Mrs Jones called.

"Me and Nana are going to do some colouring in. Look Mummy, I've got my mermaid book."

"That sounds nice," Mrs Jones said. "Are you OK there, Mum? Are you sure you don't need a break from playing with Ella?"

The older lady smiled. "Perhaps I do, but it's fine, really. I don't get to see the little ones all that often." She sat on the couch beside Ella.

"Actually," Harrie interrupted. "Can I ask you a few questions, Mrs…"

Ella's grandmother stood up. "You can call me Betty, dear."

"OK, Betty. We're still trying to find out what happened to Mum's bracelet yesterday. Did you see anyone or anything?"

"No, I'm afraid I didn't. I'm as shocked about this as anybody. I didn't actually notice your bracelet," she said to Harrie's mum, "but it's terrible that it went missing. And to think that someone may have taken it! Right here in the backyard!"

Harrie watched Betty's face carefully as she spoke. She didn't look guilty—just concerned. "Do you remember where you were when my dad fell over by the pool?"

"I do indeed." I was sitting with Ella, at the table, just beside Joan Cormack. I heard the kerfuffle and looked up to see your poor father lying on the cement."

"Were you eating at that stage?" Harrie asked.

"I was about to. I'd just taken Ella's brush and comb set into her bedroom and placed them in her toybox. I hurried outside again and sat at the table beside Ella." She paused for a moment. "That's right, I topped up her cup with cordial and was about to start eating my sausage when your poor father fell over."

"OK," Harrie said. None of this information really helped solve the case. "And you didn't notice anything else?"

"Nothing. We ate our lunch and before long we were back inside playing with… yes, playing with her dolls again."

Chapter 8

Harrie needed to gather her thoughts. "Thanks for the drink, Mrs Jones. Is it OK if Ben and I go outside for a few minutes? I'd like to have another look by the pool."

"Of course. You can both find your way, can't you?"

"Yes, we'll be fine. Come on, Ben. You can open the door."

Harrie wheeled herself out into the sunshine while Ben walked beside her.

"What are you doing?" Ben asked. "Are you looking for clues again?"

"No, I don't think there are any more clues. I just wanted a chance to think. Let's go over to the shade."

Ben sat at an outdoor setting and made space for Harrie's chair beside him.

"Ted can't possibly have taken the bracelet," Harrie said. "He was asleep the whole time."

"So, we only have two suspects."

"That's right. It must have been Mrs Jones or Betty."

"Who do you think took it?" Ben asked. "Have you got any idea?"

"No, I don't. But I want to talk through the possibilities. Firstly, we have Mrs Jones and we don't have any evidence linking her to the bracelet at all."

"Except for the things she said. She *told* your mum that she wished she had jewellery like that."

"I know, but it's not enough to convince me that she took it."

"Otherwise there's Betty and she was playing with Ella all day. I don't think she even knew your mum was wearing a bracelet."

"No," Harrie said gloomily, "she didn't. She said just now that she didn't notice Mum's bracelet. And you're right, she was with Ella all day. Playing games with her…"

Ben laughed. "And being bossed around by her…"

"And picking up all her toys…"

"That's right. She picked up her doll and her hair brush and…"

Harrie paused to think.

"What is it?" Ben asked.

"I've just had an idea! Yes, this could explain everything!"

"What?"

"Ben, I think Betty might have taken the bracelet after all!"

"But we just said she didn't even notice it."

"I know, but she might have taken it *by accident.* She was playing with Ella all day and picking up her toys and putting them away."

"Yeah. So what?"

"And she said that she didn't notice Mum's bracelet at all. She didn't know what it looked like."

"I'm still not following you."

"Don't you see? If Betty saw Mum's bracelet lying on a chair, she might have thought it was one of Ella's toys. And she might have picked it up and put it away."

"Thinking that it belonged to Ella, rather than your mum."

"That's right. Quick Ben. Wheel me inside. We have to find out!"

They hurried back, straight to the couch where Betty and Ella were sitting.

"Betty," Harrie said, "when you picked up Ella's toys yesterday, did you bring them inside and put them away?"

"Yes I did," Betty laughed. "I feel like that's what I was doing all day long." She turned to Ella and tickled her in the tummy. "You're a naughty little munchkin, aren't you?"

Ella frowned. "I'm not naughty."

"I know you're not, sweetheart. But when you're a bit older you'll learn to put your toys away. That's what good girls do."

Harrie cut back into the conversation. "Do you think you could show me where you put Ella's toys? Please? I mean, if it's OK?"

"I suppose so." Betty stood up slowly from the couch. "Come with me. Ella's room's just down the hall."

Ben pushed Harrie's chair and they followed Betty into Ella's bedroom. It was very pink. She had teddy bears, dolls and a little pink desk. In the corner there was a toybox with a few toys scattered on the carpet nearby.

"Anything I collect goes straight into the toybox, right here."

"Do you mind if I have a look?"

"What are you looking for, dear? I might be able to help you find it."

Harrie didn't answer because she was too busy digging her way down to the bottom of the toybox. "Here, take these," she said, passing teddy bears and dolls to Ben.

She reached down and ran her hand along the bottom of the toybox. And there, in the corner, she felt something that might have been a piece of jewellery. Carefully, she grasped it with her hand and pulled it out.

"Yes! Here it is! I found it!"

Ben looked at the bracelet and gave a big smile. "You did it, Harrie. Well done."

"What did you find, dear?" Betty asked.

Harrie beamed. "I found my mum's bracelet. The one she lost yesterday."

"But how did it get in here?"

Suddenly Betty understood what had happened and she brought her hands up to cover her mouth.

"Oh my… Oh no… Oh, I had no idea."

"Of course you didn't," Harrie said softly. "It was an accident. But the important thing is that we've found it. Let's all go and give it to Mum. She'll be so pleased."

When they returned to the living room Harrie said, "Mum, Mum! We found your bracelet. Here it is!"

"What? Where? Oh my goodness, you really did find it!"

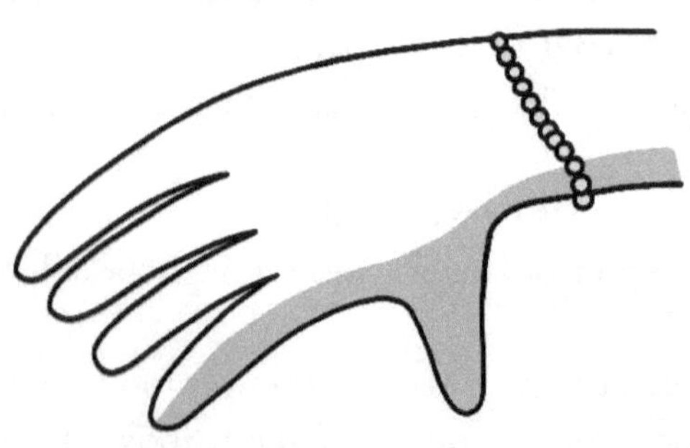

Harrie explained to her mother and Mrs Jones where the bracelet was and how it got there. Harrie's mother gave her a big hug.

"You really are a clever girl, Harrie. There's no doubt about you."

"That's wonderful news," Mrs Jones added. "Why don't we all have a special dinner tonight to celebrate. Would you like that, Susan?"

"That sounds lovely. But let's leave it up to Harrie. After all, she's the one who found the bracelet. What do you want to do for dinner, Harrie?"

"Let's go out and have pizza. Ben can come too because he helped solve the mystery. That's OK, isn't it?"

"Of course it is. You, me, your father, Ben, the Joneses and Betty—we'll all go out and have pizza for dinner."

Harrie looked around and saw that everyone was smiling. Her mother was carefully putting her bracelet on her wrist, checking that it was fastened properly. This was why she liked solving mysteries—she loved a happy ending. But best of all, she got to have pizza for dinner!

Book Two

The Lolly Shop Graffiti

Chapter 1

"Hold on tight, Ben!" Harrie called nervously. "Don't let me go!"

"Relax. I've got you. You know I'd never let anything happen to you."

Harrie took a few deep breaths. Coming down that hill always gave her butterflies but she knew she could trust Ben to look after her. There weren't many people that she trusted in this way—perhaps no-one else at all—but she could trust Ben. Once they reached the bottom of the hill she loosened her grip from the arms of her wheelchair and flopped back.

"That's better," she breathed. "Flat ground. I like being on flat ground."

"So, you don't want me to run along here and let you feel the wind in your hair?"

"No Ben," she replied quickly. "Just walk. Gee, what's got into you today?"

Even though Harrie couldn't see his face, Ben grinned. "Nothing. Nothing at all. I'll walk, I promise."

"Good. So, what amazing facts did you learn today?"

Harrie knew Ben very well as they had been best friends since they were four years old. And the thing Ben liked more than anything else was learning interesting facts and figures.

"We did learn something, actually. Mrs Hannan told us that chopsticks were invented so that people wouldn't need knives at the dinner table. Knives were considered too dangerous to be within reach when people were eating."

"We use knives all the time," Harrie argued.

"Yeah, I know. But for whatever reason the Chinese didn't want to use them for eating anymore so they chopped their food up really small, then used chopsticks to eat it."

"I love Chinese food," Harrie said. "All this talk is making me hungry."

"Well, let's stop at the lolly shop then. Have you got any money on you?"

"Yes, I've got enough to buy something to eat. What about you?"

"Me too. I've got a couple of dollars."

Harrie and Ben often called in at Mr and Mrs Anderson's lolly shop on their way home from school. The Andersons were really friendly and they had the best range of lollies in town.

Ben pushed Harrie around the corner, past the fruit shop and the pharmacy, before arriving at the lolly shop.

"Oh good," Harrie said. "They've left the front door open today. You can wheel me straight in."

Once they were inside Ben let go of Harrie's chair and she pushed the wheels herself.

"Good afternoon young Harriet and young Benjamin," Mr Anderson said with a smile. Harrie grinned. She usually didn't like people calling her by her full name—it made her feel as if she was getting into trouble—but Mr Anderson was an exception. "I hope you have both had a fine day."

"We have thanks," Harrie replied. "And how are you?"

"Oh, I'm as good as can be expected. My legs are still working and my heart is too, so that's a good combination."

Harrie didn't think of the Andersons as being really old because they were so friendly and spoke to her like an equal but when she looked closely she knew that they must be getting on a bit in years.

"We've come straight from school," Ben explained. "We left as soon as the bell rang and came straight here."

"I can see that," Mr Anderson said as he glanced at his watch. "You are my first after-school customers today. What can I get for you?"

"I might have a look around for a few minutes," Harrie said. "I haven't decided what I would like."

Ben walked up to the counter. "I know what I'm getting. I'll have a chocolate frog and a python please."

"Coming right up. And you take your time, Harrie dear. When you've made your mind up, let me know and I'll get it for you in a jiffy."

Harrie wheeled herself slowly down the aisle of chocolate bars. She saw all the usual brands that you could buy in other stores but her favourites were the chocolates that Mr and Mrs Anderson made themselves. They had over thirty different varieties including mint crunch, orange surprise, strawberry swirl and raspberry ripple. She found it very difficult to make up her mind.

Ben walked up to her. "So, what's it going to be?"

"I don't know. I really want to get banana rama, but no, I think I'll go with cherry dream and caramel fudge." Pushing herself towards the counter, Harrie placed her order.

Mr Anderson put the two squares of chocolate into a small paper bag and handed it to Harrie. "There we are. One cherry and one caramel. Anything else for today?"

"No thanks," Harrie replied as she handed her money to him.

"Well, off you go and enjoy what's left of the day."

Ben took hold of the handles of Harrie's wheelchair. "We will, thanks. See you again soon." Just as he started to turn the chair around there was a loud bang outside.

Harrie sat upright. "What was that?"

Mr Anderson hurried towards the door and went outside.

Ben pushed Harrie past the counter and out the door, pulling up beside Mr Anderson on the footpath.

"What happened?" Harrie asked.

"A young fellow, about your age, was just here but he took off so fast I couldn't see him clearly."

"Where did he go?"

Mr Anderson pointed straight ahead. "Down that way but he's gone now. He disappeared very quickly."

"Quick Ben," Harrie instructed. "Go after him. See if you can catch him."

"No no no," Mr Anderson insisted. "You won't find him. He got away too quickly. It's all right, honestly. He can't have stolen anything because he didn't come inside."

Harrie then heard another voice behind her. She turned to see that Mrs Anderson had joined them.

"What's all this?" Mrs Anderson asked. "Why are you standing out on the street?"

"Everything's fine, my love," her husband reassured her. "There was a loud noise, that's all, and a young boy ran off. But no harm has been done. Let's all go back inside."

Harrie pushed her wheels to move her chair forwards. "I'm just going to have a look around."

There was no rubbish on the ground, no broken glass. In fact, Harrie was about to agree with Mr Anderson that no damage had been done. But when she wheeled herself around the side of the shop, she saw some graffiti on the wall in bright red paint. "Whoa, what's this?" she said to herself. In a louder voice she managed to say, "Come over here, everyone. I've found something."

While they came to join her, Harrie carefully touched the edge of the graffiti and discovered that the paint was indeed wet. "It's graffiti. Someone has sprayed this on your wall. We have to find out who it was."

Chapter 2

Ben and Mr and Mrs Anderson gathered around Harrie and looked at the wall in dismay. Someone had sprayed an odd-looking shape in bright red paint.

"What do you think it's supposed to be?" Ben asked.

"A zigzag, I suppose," said Mrs Anderson.

Harrie studied it carefully. "It looks more like a lightning bolt to me."

"Kids!" Mr Anderson said in disgust. "They just don't stop and think."

Harrie and Ben glanced at each other.

"Oh no, I don't mean kids like you," Mr Anderson said quickly. "I mean kids like this." He flung his arm towards the wall.

Harrie thought for a moment. There must be something she could do to help. "Mrs Anderson," she said quietly. "Do you have a bucket we could use? I think if we act quickly we can wash the paint off without any permanent damage being done."

Mrs Anderson looked at her husband. "What do you think, love? Do we need to leave it as it is for the police?"

Harrie was shocked that they were thinking of calling the police, but a crime had been committed so she agreed that it was a reasonable possibility.

"No, I don't think calling the cops would make much difference now," Mr Anderson answered. "The little scallywag got away. No-one will be able to find him. Harrie's right. Let's clean it off while we can."

"Hang on a minute," Ben said. "Does anyone have a mobile phone?"

"Of course," Harrie said quickly. "Photos. We need photos. We can keep them as evidence."

Mr Anderson fumbled in his pockets. "Yes, here we are." He lined his phone up ready to take some pictures but Harrie noticed that his hands were shaking.

"Can I help?" she offered. "Would you like me to take them?"

Mr Anderson handed her his phone. "Thanks dear. I'm sure you'll do a better job than me. You kiddies are pretty good with phones and computers and things, aren't you?"

Harrie didn't reply but she gently took the phone and started snapping pictures.

"Ben, can you help please? Wheel me away a bit so I can get some shots from further back."

"Sure." Ben moved Harrie's chair away from the wall and Harrie took some more photos.

"There we are," she said as she handed Mr Anderson's phone back to him. "I got some close up and some with the whole wall included. Keep those on your phone in case you need them for anything."

Mrs Anderson turned around to walk back into the shop. "I'll just go and get a bucket so we can clean this off."

"Thanks love," Mr Anderson said. "And thanks to you two as well. You've been a big help today."

Harrie frowned, realising the seriousness of what had happened. "That's OK. I just hope we can find out who did this."

"I don't think we will," Mr Anderson said, shaking his head. "There's nothing more we can do."

"Harrie will find something," Ben said, trying to make Mr Anderson feel a bit better. "She's very good at solving mysteries."

Harrie shook her head. "This isn't really a mystery."

"Yes it is. We need to find out who sprayed the graffiti on the wall."

Harrie nodded as a little wave of excitement rippled through her. "I'll give it my best anyway. I'll go home and think about it tonight and call in tomorrow if I get any good ideas. And Ben will help, won't you?"

"Of course I will."

"Well, thank you," Mr Anderson replied. "You're good kids, both of you. But to be honest, once we wash this off I'd rather put the whole business behind me. Nothing was stolen and no-one was hurt, so I should be grateful for that."

Harrie turned and saw Mrs Anderson walking towards them, carrying a bucket of steamy water. "All right. Let me put this down. Make some room so I can start scrubbing."

"Here," Ben said as he stepped forward. "Let me do that."

"Oh, you're a good boy. Thanks very much."

It didn't take long for Ben to clean the wall. Once he had removed the paint, Mr Anderson brought a hose around and rinsed the suds and red streaks off the wall. "There. It looks as good as new. Did you know that I painted the lettering on this wall myself?"

"Really?" Harrie replied. "It must have been a long time ago."

"It was. Forty-two years to be exact. We bought this store just after we married and have been running it ever since."

"Gee wiz," Ben said. "My mum's thirty-nine and my dad's forty-one, so you owned this shop before they were even born."

"That's right. We've seen generations of kiddies grow up. But enough of all that. You two had better be on your way. I can't thank you enough for all your help today."

Harrie smiled. "Anyone would have done the same."

"I really must go now," Mr Anderson said. "I just saw a couple of customers walk in. Thanks again."

"That's OK," Harrie said. "We'll call in tomorrow."

Ben started pushing Harrie towards home. "Poor Mr Anderson," he said as he started to eat his chocolate frog. "That's an awful thing to happen. And he's such a nice man."

"I know. I think he was quite upset about it. Did you notice how his hands were shaking?"

"Yeah, I did. We have to help them, Harrie. We have to find out who did it."

"I know. I'll do my best. I'll think about it tonight and see what ideas I get."

"Me too. I've got some homework so I won't hang around at your place today. But I'll pick you up at the usual time in the morning and we can talk about how to catch the graffiti artist."

Harrie smiled. "Sounds good. I'll see you in the morning."

Chapter 3

Harrie breezed through the first two sections without any problems but when she reached Part 3 she really started to slow down. *What is six times seven?* she asked herself. Her class had learnt their six times tables a few weeks ago but Harrie now had a mental block.

Every Wednesday morning all the students in her school did a Speed Test. It consisted of one hundred mental arithmetic questions and each section was more difficult than the one before it. Harrie could usually answer most questions in the first half of the test, but the later sections were based on work for older students, so she didn't try these at all. With a time limit of five minutes she felt it was better to concentrate on the questions that she had a chance of getting right.

"Time!" her teacher—Mr Corey—called in a loud voice. The students swapped papers and marked each other's tests as Mr Corey read out the answers.

Harrie was marking Katie Mannion's test and was impressed to see that she had answered nearly every question on the paper. Katie was one of the cleverest students in Harrie's class and Harrie smiled as she returned her paper to her with a mark of eighty-nine written clearly in red pen at the top.

As he did every week, Mr Corey walked around the class and wrote down everyone's marks. Then, continuing with his weekly practice, he scanned his list and read out the top three marks. Harrie knew what to expect. It was the same few students who got the highest marks all the time. Harrie's name was never read out because she usually scored somewhere between fifty and sixty, but she was happy for those who did well each week.

"So," Mr Corey said in a loud voice, "in first place today we have Becky Simons." Harrie clapped along with the rest of the class but she was somewhat surprised at the result. Noah Wilson usually came first but this week Becky had beaten him.

"And in second place we have Toby Smythe." Harrie clapped, convinced that Noah would come third.

"And finally we have Katie Mannion in third place."

Harrie was amazed. She looked at Noah and saw that he had his head down. He was a quiet boy who didn't say much in class but he usually got top marks in everything.

Oh well, Harrie thought to herself. Maybe he's just having a bad day.

"Good effort everyone," Mr Corey said from the front of the classroom. "And remember, you can always do better next week, so keep practising. Now we are going to have fifteen minutes of silent reading before I give you your new spelling words. Please take out your books and read quietly."

Harrie opened her desk and picked up her book. She tried to read but found it too difficult to concentrate. Her mind went straight back to Mr and Mrs Anderson and what had happened the previous afternoon. She had planned to give the matter some thought at home in the evening but after dinner there was a good movie on tv and she ended up watching that instead.

She remembered that Mr Anderson said he had seen a boy running away. Unfortunately Harrie didn't see the boy herself but she felt pretty sure that he would have been the person who had painted the graffiti. It would have been better if they had arrived outside more quickly, but as it was, Mr Anderson only caught a brief glimpse of the boy.

Harrie also pondered the shape of the graffiti itself. She quietly opened her desk again, not wanting Mr Corey to hear her, and took out a writing pad. She drew a sketch of what the graffiti had looked like. It was an odd shape and something about it niggled at Harrie's mind. Had she seen this shape before? There was just something about it that was familiar.

At recess time she met up with Ben and walked across the playground with him. There was a rough ball game of some kind being played nearby so they moved away and found some seats in the shade so that Ben could sit down. As Harrie started to eat her biscuits, she told Ben what she had been thinking about in class and how she thought the graffiti looked familiar to her.

"It's funny you should say that," he said. "I think I've seen the tag somewhere too."

"You do?"

"Yeah, I think so but I don't know where."

"Ben, what do you mean by tag?" Harrie asked.

"That's what it's called. It's a tag. If someone does graffiti they usually have their own tag and paint that shape all over the place."

"Kind of like a signature?"

"Yes, exactly. Each person, or each graffiti artist, has his or her own tag."

"Thanks Ben. That's a great help. I'll look up tags later today and find out some more about them."

Just then they heard a crashing sound and looked up to see the football bounce off the window of one of the classrooms.

"Gee," Harrie said. "Those boys had better be careful. They nearly broke the window."

"Don't worry about the window," Ben said. "They nearly smashed the security camera. That would cost way more than a window."

"Oh my gosh, Ben!" Harrie exclaimed. "You're brilliant!"

Ben shook his head in confusion. "What? Everyone knows cameras are expensive."

"I'm not talking about the camera. Well, I am actually."

"Harrie, you're not making any sense. What's going on?"

"Security cameras. I've been racking my brain trying to think how we can figure out who vandalised the Anderson's shop yesterday and you just gave me the answer!"

"Do you mean CCTV?"

"That's exactly what I mean."

"But I don't know if they have cameras at their store."

"Neither do I. But we can find out, can't we? It's the best idea we've had so far."

Chapter 4

On the way back to their classrooms, Harrie and Ben stopped at the lockers to put their lunch boxes away. All the children in their year level had a locker in this area, so Harrie waited for a minute or so until it wasn't as crowded so that she could get her wheelchair in close enough. When she backed away she noticed how messy the lockers were. At some schools lockers had doors on them and students needed a key to open them, but at Harrie's school they were 'open lockers', perhaps more like pigeon holes. Harrie would never put anything valuable in there but at least she had a space where she could leave things. Most people's lockers were stuffed full—some even had rubbish in them—and Harrie wondered how they could find what they needed. She ran her hand along the top of the lockers and down the side, feeling a small ridge that had been dug out of the wood. She peered closely and saw that someone had carved into the wood a message that said 'I love Ollie.' Harrie shook her head. If Mr Corey knew this was here he would be very disappointed. Then, just before she turned to leave, she noticed something else on the side of the lockers. It was a shape drawn on in marker pen. Her jaw dropped as she realised what it was—it was the same tag that had been spray painted onto the wall of the lolly shop.

Her mind raced as she thought about what this might mean. These lockers were just for the children in her year level, so the person who drew it must be in either her class or Ben's class! She wondered if perhaps it could have been there for a long time—maybe from last year or the year before—but she doubted that because the cleaners would have scrubbed it off by now.

She hurried to her classroom, not wanting to be too late, but she couldn't concentrate on geography because her mind was filled with finding out who the mysterious graffiti artist was. When lunchtime finally arrived she wheeled herself out into the yard as quickly as she could, trying to find Ben. She made her way down the ramp and as she turned the corner she crashed into someone who was coming in the opposite direction.

"Oh my goodness!" Harrie said. "I'm so sorry. I didn't see you."

She had run into Alex Simpson, an unpleasant boy in Ben's class who always had a scowl on his face.

"Watch where you're going!" he snarled.

Although Harrie was sorry that she had run into Alex, she didn't appreciate being spoken to in that tone of voice. And besides, perhaps it was Alex who ran into her. It wasn't all her fault.

"I said I was *sorry*," she said as she wheeled herself away quickly. Once Alex had walked off, Harrie looked towards him. He had dark hair and was neatly dressed but he always looked angry. He was a bully too. Harrie knew this because she had been in his class last year and had seen the way he treated other students. One time he stole two dollars from Becky Simons. Becky had brought the money to school to spend at the canteen and it had gone missing one morning while the class was doing story-writing. When Becky couldn't find it at the start of lunch, she burst into tears and Harrie patted her on the back and did her best to help her feel better. Harrie never found out exactly how Alex got the money, but she knew it was him because she overheard him bragging to his friends. Even though Alex was so awful, a lot of the other boys looked up to him and joined in with his antics whenever they could.

Harrie was suddenly distracted from her thoughts as Ben ran towards her.

"Harrie," he called. "I need to talk to you. I found something just now!"

Ben sat down on a seat and Harrie pulled up beside him. "I just went to the toilets," Ben said, slightly out of breath, "and you won't believe what I saw!"

"What?" Harrie asked.

"I saw the tag! It was right there in front of me, drawn on the wall."

"The lightning bolt tag?" Harrie asked, just to make sure she understood correctly.

"Yeah, like at the lolly shop. The exact same one."

"I saw it too."

"You did?" Ben asked. "Where?"

"On the side of the lockers. It was drawn on with a Sharpie or something like that."

"This was too. The one in the toilets, I mean. We're getting closer Harrie, we really are. You're going to find out who it was, I know you will."

"I hope so. I suppose we have a few clues now. Let's think about what we know."

"It's got to be a boy," Ben said, "because it was in the boys' toilets."

"That's a start. It rules out half the school." They both laughed. Clearly, they still had a long way to go. "But it's also someone in our year level because it was on the lockers."

"OK, so a boy in our year level. That's one in about thirty people. And it wasn't me, I swear, so about one in twenty-nine people. That's good progress—we just have to figure out which boy it was."

"And we haven't even seen the CCTV footage yet," Harrie added. "I really hope the Andersons have a camera installed. It will be a huge help."

"We'll go there straight after school as planned. I've got a good feeling about this, Harrie. We're going to find out who did it."

Chapter 5

Ben appeared at Harrie's classroom almost as soon as the bell rang. "Come on Harrie," he whispered, trying not to attract Mr Corey's attention. "Hurry up."

Harrie quickly put her pencil case in her bag, balanced her bag on her lap and wheeled herself towards the door.

"You got here quickly today," she commented.

"Yeah, of course. We want to go to the lolly shop to see if we can find some more clues, don't we?"

"We sure do," Harrie agreed.

Ben pushed her out the school gate and down the street. They arrived at the Andersons' shop even earlier than the previous day.

"Hi Mr and Mrs Anderson," Harrie said as she wheeled herself inside. Mr Anderson was stacking the shelves and Mrs Anderson was writing something in a book behind the counter.

"Hello hello," Mr Anderson replied. His wife smiled and waved. "What can we get for the two of you today?"

Harrie looked around and noticed that there were no other customers in the store. "We don't want to buy anything, we want to talk to you about yesterday. You haven't found out who did the graffiti, have you?"

Mrs Anderson shook her head. "No, we haven't got any further with that and I don't expect that we will. These things happen sometimes and we were lucky that we dealt with it straight away."

"But you can't give up," Harrie insisted. "We must find out who did it. We *must.*"

Mr Anderson walked over and spoke to Harrie in a gentle tone. "We don't have anything to go on, love. I saw a young fella run away, but I barely saw him to be honest. I certainly couldn't identify him. I wouldn't even come close."

Harrie was determined to help out in any way she could. "Well, Ben and I have found out a bit more. In fact, we know it was a boy from our school."

"You do?" Mr Anderson said with surprise. "But how… I mean… I couldn't even tell you what he was wearing. I don't know if he had a uniform on or not. I really only caught a tiny glimpse of him."

Harrie smiled. "So, like I said, we're going to help. He definitely goes to our school and we know something else too."

"You do?" Mr Anderson said again.

"Yes I do. He's in either my class or Ben's class."

Mrs Anderson walked out from behind the counter and stood beside Harrie's wheelchair. "I know you're trying to help, Harrie dear, but you really must be careful of accusing people who you know."

Harrie began to feel frustrated. She felt like she wasn't getting anywhere. She had to make the Andersons believe her. "Let me explain everything more slowly. Do you remember the shape that was painted on your wall yesterday?"

Mr and Mrs Anderson both nodded. "It was a funny kind of zigzag," Mr Anderson said.

"That's right. This morning Ben saw the same shape—exactly the same shape—on the wall in the boys' toilets at school."

Mrs Anderson gasped and covered her mouth with her hand.

"And," Harrie continued, "I saw the shape drawn on the side of the lockers at school. The lockers right outside our classrooms—that's how I know it had to be someone in our year level."

Mr Anderson pulled a chair over so he could sit beside Harrie. "You mean to tell us that you saw the same shape at your school? Twice?"

"Yes," Ben said. "Both Harrie and I thought it looked familiar and now we know why. But we've got an important question for you."

"Fire away," Mr Anderson said.

Harrie turned her chair and looked up into the four corners of the ceiling. "We're wondering if you have any security cameras in here."

"We did have once upon a time," Mr Anderson replied, "but they haven't worked for many years."

Harrie looked at Ben and saw that he was just as disappointed as she felt.

"That's right," Mrs Anderson explained. "We used to have them in here but that was a long time ago. All we have now is the outside one."

Harrie's face immediately brightened. "Outside is what we need! Where outside? Is it near the wall that was graffitied?"

Mr Anderson pushed himself up out of the chair. "It's out the front of the shop. I don't think it captures the wall that we need but let's have a look, shall we?"

Mr Anderson led the way, followed by Harrie, Ben and last of all Mrs Anderson. Together, they looked up at the camera. Harrie noticed that it was covered in cobwebs but otherwise seemed to be in quite good condition.

Ben stood underneath the camera, gazing up at it. "I don't think it would have filmed the boy as he painted the graffiti, but you should have some footage of him running away. The camera points that way—can everyone see? So, as the boy ran past the newsagent next door, he would have been caught on film."

Harrie looked at Mr Anderson and then Mrs Anderson. "Do you have the footage? Can we watch it?"

"Oh my," Mr Anderson said, scratching his head. "I haven't used that machine in over fifteen years. I'm not sure I remember how it works."

"I'll work it out," Ben said. "If you can show me where it is, I'll figure it out from there."

Chapter 6

Ben pulled up a chair and Harrie rolled in beside him. They were in the Anderson's office—a tiny table covered in a mess of papers, books and other odds and ends.

"Here," Mr Anderson offered. "Let me get some of this junk out of your way."

Ben pushed his chair back and Mr Anderson stepped into the small space provided to pick up an armful of clutter from the table.

"Push that button there so the screen comes on and I'll see if I can find the right cord."

Following Mr Anderson's instructions, Ben pressed the button at the bottom of the screen. Harrie hadn't seen a computer as old as this in her whole life and she wondered if it would really work properly. After a minute or so the screen lit up but all Harrie could see was a fuzzy grey pattern. "There's no picture," she said.

"Hold your horses," Mr Anderson replied. "I have to plug this in first. Here, let me see, yes I think this is the right one."

He held a cord in his hand and bent over awkwardly to plug it into the back of the computer. As soon as he did, Harrie saw a clear image of the footpath out the front of the shop come up on the screen.

"It works!" she exclaimed.

Mr Anderson cleared his throat. "I should hope so. That's what it's there for. Mind you, I haven't used it in so long, I wouldn't be surprised if it had called it quits long before now."

"How do we get back to yesterday afternoon?" Ben asked.

"It shouldn't be too hard," Mr Anderson replied as he pushed his glasses up his nose, closer to his eyes. "Maybe I just press *Rewind* here." He tapped his finger on the *Rewind* button and the image started to roll backwards.

"If you press it again it might rewind faster," Harrie suggested.

Mr Anderson pressed the button again and it rewound twice as quickly as before.

"That's great," Ben said. "It even shows the date and time at the top of the screen. We're already back as far as ten o'clock this morning so it shouldn't take much longer."

Harrie felt excitement bubble up inside her. She finally felt like they were making some real progress. It was quite a breakthrough to find the tag at school but watching this video might actually identify the graffiti artist. "Hey Ben," she said. "Have you made any notes on this case in your notebook?"

"Of course I have. It's right here."

He pulled his notebook—which he carried everywhere with him—out of his pocket and showed Harrie what he had written. "I drew a rough picture of the lightning bolt. It's not very good but it's enough to help me remember. I wrote the date and the time when it happened, I made a note that it was painted with red paint and also that we took photos using Mr Anderson's phone."

"Nice one," Harrie smiled. She knew she could rely on Ben to do things properly.

Ben turned the page of his notebook. "Then today," he continued, "I added that I found the tag in the boys' toilets and that you saw it on the side of the lockers."

"And hopefully soon we'll have some more information to add," Harrie said.

"Yep. Look, we're nearly there. It happened at 3:42 yesterday afternoon, so I'll stop it rewinding, right about, now." He picked up the remote that Mr Anderson had left sitting on the table and pressed *Play*. The time said 3:39 so it was only a few minutes before the incident happened.

Harrie removed her eyes from the screen and looked directly at Ben. "You said the time was 3:42. What did you mean by that exactly?"

"That's what time it was when we heard the bang and went outside."

"When the boy ran away?"

"Yeah, I guess."

"So, at 3:39 or 3:40 where it's actually up to now, whoever it was would have been there painting the wall."

"I hadn't thought of that," Ben replied, "but yes, he must have been."

Harrie felt tingles wash over her whole body. She was watching footage of the street outside the lolly shop at the exact time it was being vandalised. But she couldn't see anything—not yet, anyway. All she could see was people walking past in both directions.

Everyone had their eyes glued to the screen. After another couple of minutes they saw a figure running away with his back to the camera.

"Play it again," Harrie urged. "He disappeared so quickly. I want to see it again."

Ben rewound the tape and pressed *Play*. Paying more attention this time, Harrie saw a boy with black hair running. "I wish he had turned around," she muttered, "then we could have seen his face. Play it once more, Ben. Will it go in slow motion?"

"I don't think so. It's too old."

They watched the video one final time and Ben paused it when the boy was fully in view. "That's about the best shot we have of him."

"He's definitely got black hair," Harrie said. "And he doesn't look particularly tall either. About average height, I'd say."

Ben nodded. "Yeah, about my height I reckon. Let me write that down. Black hair. Average height."

Harrie frowned as she pulled all the clues together in her mind. "So, it's a boy in our year with black hair, who's not too tall and not too short. Surely that doesn't leave us with too many suspects. Let me think. The only boy in my class with black hair is Noah Wilson. There's also Billy Tomlinson but he's too short. It definitely wasn't Billy in the video. What about your class, Ben?"

"The only two I can think of are Tony Morris and Alex Simpson. I'll check tomorrow in case I've forgotten anyone, but I think that's all."

"Ugh," Harrie shuddered. "I wouldn't be surprised if it was Alex. He's a nasty piece of work. He ran into me earlier today and didn't even apologise."

Ben smiled.

"What's so funny?" Harrie asked.

"Nothing. I'm just smiling because you're usually really careful not to jump to conclusions."

Harrie sighed. "You're right. I don't have any *proof* that it was Alex. I just wouldn't be surprised, that's all."

As they stood up to leave, Harrie heard the bell on the back of the shop door tinkle, indicating that a customer was walking in. "Someone's here," she said. "We'll be on our way so that you can serve your customer."

"Thanks again kids," Mr Anderson said. "I really do appreciate your help and I hope that what we saw on film today helps us figure out who did it."

As Harrie steered herself around the counter and entered the shop again, she lifted her head to look where she was going and froze in shock. She reached out and grabbed hold of Ben's arm. They looked at each other but didn't dare say a word. The customer who had just entered the shop was Alex Simpson.

Chapter 7

Harrie's heart beat so fast it felt like it was going to jump right out of her chest. She kept her head down and wheeled herself out of the store as quickly as she could. Once she was outside Ben started to push her and she sank back in her chair.

"What was Alex doing there?" she asked furiously.

"No idea," Ben said. "Maybe he wants some lollies or something."

"For someone who's so smart, sometimes you can be really thick, Ben!"

"Huh?"

"I'm sorry. I shouldn't have spoken to you like that. But it was Alex. He fits the description of the graffiti artist."

"Yeah but so do at least two other boys."

"But what if it *was* him? Why do you think he would come back?"

Ben didn't have a clue where Harrie was going with this line of questioning, so without saying anything, he let her continue.

"My guess is that he came back to gloat! To strut around the shop that he vandalised, thinking no-one knows that it was him."

"But we don't know. We know it *could* have been him, but that's all."

"I've just got a funny feeling about this. He picks on kids younger than him and he never does any work in class. I don't know why so many boys hang around him. They treat him like he's some sort of king. But he's horrible, he really is. I know what you're going to say Ben, and you're right. We need to look into it further, and we will. But as far as I'm concerned, Alex is our number one suspect."

At school the next day, Harrie and Ben made a plan about what they should do next. They were confident that the graffiti artist was one of three boys—Alex Simpson, Tony Morris or Noah Wilson. Even though Harrie still felt that it was most likely Alex, she knew they had to find good reasons to eliminate the other two boys from their investigation.

"Maybe we should focus on Tony for a while," Ben suggested. "We could follow him around at lunchtime and see if we get any ideas."

"Sounds good," Harrie replied. Tony was a friendly boy and he loved to play jokes on people. Harrie knew this because she had been in the same class as him several times. He was what some people would refer to as the *class clown*. Last year he played a prank on their teacher—Mrs Wayward. One day when Mrs Wayward had collected their story writing, Tony snuck up the front and smeared a strip of glue down the middle of each piece of paper. That night when Mrs Wayward wanted to read through the stories, she couldn't separate them because they were all stuck together! The whole class tried not to burst out laughing the next day when Mrs Wayward made up the excuse that she had lost their writing. She said she left them in a café after school, and when she went back to look for them they'd disappeared! Harrie hadn't seen Tony play the prank but word had spread so quickly around the class that she knew it had to be true.

Tony was usually harmless though. At lunchtime Harrie and Ben watched him kick the footy on the oval with a group of boys. They noticed that he was wearing long sleeves.

"Why would he be wearing a hoodie on a day like today?" Harrie asked. "It's stinking hot."

"Especially running around like that," Ben added.

Something didn't seem right to Harrie. No-one else had a warm top on, so why did Tony? She ate her sandwich while she watched the boys run around. Someone kicked the ball high up in the air and it flew over towards them. Harrie watched as Tony ran towards it, leaving the others behind. When the ball hit the ground, he dived on it and picked it up, only a few metres from where Harrie and Ben were sitting.

"Ben," she whispered urgently. "Did you see that?"

"The dive?"

"No, not the dive." Harrie spoke in a normal voice again now that Tony was out of earshot. "Tony's arms had red paint on them. I was trying to work out why he had red streaks on his hands when I noticed it was all over his arms as well."

"You don't think…" Ben started but Harrie cut him off.

"Red paint! It's just like the paint on the lolly shop wall."

"Graffiti artists usually use spray paint," Ben added.

"Well, whatever it is, it's all over his hands and arms. He's one of our suspects and this doesn't look good for him."

"You're right," Ben said. "It doesn't look good at all."

"There's no point watching this game anymore. Let's go back to the main building."

As they walked past the doorway that led into the main hall, Harrie felt a blast of air-conditioning. "Let's go inside for a few minutes, Ben. It's nice and cool in there."

Ben turned Harrie's chair around and pushed her inside. "Look," he said, "they're having a practice match of basketball—girls versus boys."

"I hope the girls win."

Harrie watched the game as she recovered from the heat outside. It seemed both teams were taking the game very seriously and she looked up to the score board to see that the boys were leading, thirty-eight to thirty-five.

"Come on girls!" she called. "You can do it!"

"Did you know," Ben began, "how much the rules of basketball have changed over the years?"

"What rules?" Harrie asked.

"Dribbling, for one. Players are allowed to dribble the ball now but that's a relatively new thing. Well, since 1897 anyway."

"Really? How did they move if they couldn't dribble?"

"They had to pass the ball to someone else before they could move. Once they caught the ball they had to stay still."

"That's the same as netball then."

Ben shrugged. "Similar, I guess. That's what I read though. And another thing, these days teams must have five players, but in the past there wasn't any limit to how big your side could be. People often played basketball with fifteen or twenty on their team."

"No way."

Harrie liked hearing Ben's facts. He had an amazing memory and he was always reading and learning random bits of information.

"Look over there," Ben said, pointing to the far end of the court. "Who's that player in the green top?"

Harrie's mouth dropped open. "It's Alex. Alex Simpson."

"That's twice we've seen him unexpectedly."

"Write it in your notebook, Ben."

"Write what?"

"Write down that Alex plays basketball. It may be nothing but I've got a feeling that it's something we should remember."

Chapter 8

"Hurry up everyone," Mr Corey said in a loud voice. "Come in and take your seats. I know you'd rather still be outside having your lunch but it's time to settle. Yes, you too Anthony. Quick sticks. Come and sit down."

Harrie opened her desk and rearranged her books. After lunch on Wednesdays her class usually did art, so she knew she wouldn't need any writing books for the rest of the day.

"One," Mr Corey called. Harrie stopped fiddling and folded her arms. Her teacher was counting to three and if anyone was still making a noise by the time he got to three, there would be trouble. "Two." Harrie didn't know what kind of trouble because it hadn't happened yet. "Three." The class was silent.

"That's better. Much better. This afternoon we're going to get the paints out and each of you is going to create a bushland scene. There are three things I want you to include in your picture. The first is you must make it clear what season it is. Think of the colouring and the background you would use for either summer, autumn, winter or spring. When I look at the finished product I should be able to tell what the season is.

"Secondly, I want you to include an animal in your painting. It can be any animal you like—from a kangaroo to a caterpillar—it doesn't matter as long as there is an animal. And thirdly, I want to see a native Australian plant. We have been studying these over the past few weeks so this is a good chance to show what you know. Are there any questions?"

Nobody raised their hand so Mr Corey quickly moved on. "Right. Let's get organised then. One person from each row can come and get the paint then I'd like everyone to start without a fuss."

Harrie worked hard on her painting. She chose to paint her grandmother's backyard because it was out in the bush and it gave her something familiar to focus on. The animal she chose was a magpie and she painted it sitting on the branch of a gum tree. It wasn't exactly a bush scene but Harrie thought that if she left out the fence, Mr Corey wouldn't know the difference.

The time flew by and Harrie finished her painting just ten minutes before the bell was due to ring at the end of the day. She laid it carefully on her desk and wheeled herself down the back of the classroom to wash her pallet in the sink.

After wiping it dry with a rag, she bent forward to put the pallet away in the cupboard. Just at that moment something caught her eye. It was the tag again! There was no doubt about it. Right there in front of her on the inside of the cupboard door was the unusual lightning-shaped zigzag, this time in blue pen.

"How can it be here?" Harrie asked herself. Making her way back towards her desk, she thought hard about what this meant. Did it mean that the graffiti artist was in her class? That narrowed it down to Noah Wilson because the other two suspects were in Ben's class. But Noah didn't seem the type of boy who would do something that was so blatantly against school rules. He was a nice boy, a quiet boy. And until recently, he had been doing very well in class. She had noticed that he seemed distracted lately but she didn't think he would ever do something as serious as this.

Harrie wondered what she should do next. Should she confront Noah and ask him if he did this or should she talk it over with Ben first? She wished Ben was with her, right here right now. He would know what to do.

"Hurry up everyone," Mr Corey called. "The bell will ring soon and I want this classroom spotless."

Harrie looked on the floor beneath her desk and found that it was all tidy. Her gaze drifted over towards Noah.

He was sitting still, looking absently at something on the opposite side of the room.

"Right," Harrie muttered to herself. "Let's do this." She turned her chair around and wheeled herself over to Noah's desk. "Hi Noah," she said when she arrived.

"Uh, hi Harrie."

"I wondered if I could have a quick word. I want to show you something down the back."

"Sure," Noah replied. "Shall I… push you?"

"No, I'm fine. Just come with me."

Harrie wasn't able to move very quickly because there were children rushing in all directions, particularly down the back of the classroom. "It's just down here a bit further."

Before they reached the cupboard the bell rang to mark the end of the school day. Mr Corey raised his voice again. "Right everyone. Make sure you have all your belongings and off you go. I'll see you tomorrow."

Harrie knew she had to hurry. "It's just here, Noah."

She opened the cupboard door and pointed to the tag that she had found a few minutes earlier. "I was wondering if you knew anything about this."

Harrie looked at Noah and just as he noticed that she was pointing to the tag, a panicked look crept across his face. He immediately turned around and ran out the door.

Chapter 9

The next morning Harrie and Ben discussed the mystery of the lolly shop graffiti on their way to school. Of course Harrie had already told Ben about what had happened with Noah but they still didn't know who the real culprit was.

"The thing is," Ben said, "we have quite a convincing clue for each of our suspects."

"Exactly," Harrie cut in. "Alex turned up at the shop the very next day, Tony has red paint all over him and I found the tag in my classroom—or rather, Noah's classroom."

"It could have been any of them," Ben stated.

"I know. So, I've decided that today we need to do our best to find out who did it. We'll talk to each of them if we have to, but we've got to get to the bottom of this."

When they arrived at school they wandered around the playground slowly, looking out for the three boys. Mr White was on yard duty and he nodded at Harrie and Ben as they passed him.

"I've never really met Mr White properly," Harrie said to Ben.

"Me either. He teaches the older kids."

"And he coaches the basketball team."

"Harrie!" Ben exclaimed. "Did you hear what you just said?"

"What do you mean?"

"I mean, you said he coaches the basketball team. And Alex is in the basketball team!"

"Oh yes!" Harrie said excitedly. Then she frowned. "But it doesn't really help us, does it?"

"It might. I think we should talk to him. Come on, let's go."

Harrie gathered her thoughts. She would be grateful for any more clues that she could get. "Good morning Mr White," she began.

"Good morning," he replied. "You're Harrie Taylor, aren't you?"

Harrie nodded.

"And what's your name, young man?"

"I'm Ben Scobey."

"It's a pleasure to meet you. What can I do for you?"

Harrie fumbled with her fingers. She didn't really know what to ask. "We were just wondering if you know a boy called Alex Simpson."

"I do indeed. He's in the basketball squad. Not a bad player either. What about him?"

"We were wondering…" Harrie had to think quickly. She needed to come up with something to say. "We just wanted to ask if you thought he was very good at basketball."

Harrie cringed. It was the only thing she could think of.

"Like I said, he's not bad. It would help if he was a bit taller but he works hard. I'll give him that."

"Does he always turn up to training and matches and everything?" Ben asked.

"Sure he does. Why, at Monday's training session he was the first to arrive and one of the last to leave."

"Monday?" Harrie said quickly. "Did you say he had basketball training on Monday?"

"Yes, just like every week. What exactly is it that you two want?"

"Oh nothing," Ben said. "We're just curious, that's all. Alex is in my class and I heard he was pretty good at basketball."

Harrie smiled, grateful that Ben had been able to keep the conversation on track.

"One more thing, Mr White," Harrie said. "What time was Monday's training practice?"

"Straight after school, of course. No different to any other week. 3:30 to 4:30. Now, I must be going. I'm on duty and I need to check the bus area. Have a good day." And with that, Mr White briskly walked away.

Ben wheeled Harrie over to the seats and sat down. "That rules Alex out then."

"Yes it does," Harrie agreed. "He was at basketball practice the whole time. That's a pretty good alibi."

"So, it only leaves Tony and Noah. Who do you think did it?"

Harrie shrugged. "I don't know but we'll find out. There's no time now because the bell's about to ring but meet me at recess and we'll decide what to do next."

Luckily, Tony Morris was one of the first people that Harrie and Ben saw at recess. Just like before, he wore a long-sleeved top, even though the weather was so hot.

"Tony!" Harrie called. "Can we talk to you for a moment?"

"G'day guys," he said with a grin. "What's happening?"

"This might sound strange but is it OK if you pull up the sleeves of your hoodie a bit? I want to check something."

Tony didn't seem at all bothered to do as Harrie asked. "It's such a pain," he said. "I'm only wearing it because I've got this red paint on my arms and I can't wash it off."

"Yeah," Ben agreed. "It *is* pretty hot."

"You're telling *me*," Tony said. "I'm sweltering. But if Mrs Hannan sees this, I could be in big trouble. And there's no need for that, is there?"

"How did you get paint on you?" Harrie asked.

"By helping my dad out at home. He's redecorating the front yard and I've been helping him paint. I don't tell many people this but he's a mad keen Swans supporter and he wants the railing at home to be red and white. It's mental if you ask me."

"Swans, as in the AFL?" Ben checked.

"That's right. Sydney Swans."

"And you obviously got the job of painting the red bits," Harrie confirmed.

Tony nodded. "And the stupid stuff won't wash off! Believe me, I've tried. It's just starting to get flaky, so hopefully it'll be gone in a few more days."

"Oh well," Harrie said. "Thanks for your help."

"No worries. See you round."

"What do you think?" Harrie asked Ben as soon as Tony had walked away.

"It looked to me like he was telling the truth. He didn't seem nervous or anything."

"I agree. And it's easy enough to check out his story. He lives in Mair St so we can go past his place on our way home from school. It's not far out of the way."

"No problem," Ben said. "There won't be too many houses freshly painted in red and white."

Chapter 10

As Harrie expected, Tony had been telling the truth. With both he and Alex eliminated from her investigation, the only suspect left was Noah.

She and Ben arrived at school early the next morning, hoping to find Noah before class began.

"Look," Ben said, pointing towards the school gate. "That's him, isn't it?"

"Sure is. Wait until he comes over. There's no need to go chasing after him."

Noah walked towards the classroom but when he saw Harrie looking straight at him, he quickly turned and went the other way.

"Wait Noah! Ben and I just want to talk to you."

They hurried after him and caught up outside the next block of classrooms. "We're trying to work something out and we thought you might be able to help us. Do you think you could do that?"

"I s'pose so." Noah looked down and fiddled awkwardly with his fingers.

Harrie spoke with a gentle voice. "Remember yesterday afternoon when we were packing the art things away…"

"I don't want to talk about that."

"It's OK," Harrie assured him. "I'm not going to tell Mr Corey. I promise."

Noah lifted his head a little and Harrie took that as a sign that it was OK to continue. "I need you to tell me the truth, Noah. Did you draw that tag on the cupboard?"

Noah didn't reply but after a few seconds he slowly nodded his head.

"And we found the same thing on the lockers. Did you do that one too?"

Again Noah nodded.

"What about in the boys' toilets?" Ben asked.

"Yes it was me, all right? Are you happy now? Can I go?"

"We just want to know why. Why did you draw your tag in those places? If Mr Corey found out you'd get detention for weeks."

"You promised you wouldn't tell him," Noah said in a rush.

"And I'll keep my promise. I won't tell him. But only if you help us out a little further."

"What do you mean? How can I help?"

"We want to know why you did it."

"I can't talk about this stuff," Noah said. He looked really embarrassed.

"I don't think you've got much of a choice. We know what you did, so you need to cooperate with us."

Noah's shoulders slumped. "It's because… it's because I haven't got any friends. I thought if I did something like that, the tough guys would take notice of me and maybe let me hang out with them."

"The tough guys?" Harrie asked. "Who are they?"

"You know, Alex and Callum and all them. They're good at sport and they always look like they're having fun. I just wanted to be more like them."

"I'll tell you what I think," Harrie said. "I think you're way better than them. You're smart. You're good at maths and English and those other boys stir up trouble all the time. Do you really want to be friends with them?"

"It's better than no friends at all. But I've said enough. I want to go now."

"Just one more thing," Harrie insisted. "We noticed your tag on the wall of the lolly shop. That's pretty serious, Noah."

His face fell once more.

"It was you, wasn't it?"

This time he had tears in his eyes.

"Nothing else was working. I thought maybe if I did something really bad…"

"That Alex and his mates would notice," Ben said. "We get the picture."

"But it's really serious," Harrie continued.

"I know," Noah muttered. "And I'm sorry. I really am."

"We're not the ones you need to be sorry to," Harrie said. "The Andersons own that store. They're the ones you have to apologise to."

As difficult as it was for Noah, he agreed to go with Harrie and Ben after school to see Mr and Mrs Anderson.

"And who do we have here?" Mr Anderson greeted them cheerfully. "You've brought a friend with you today?"

"Kind of," Harrie said. "This is Noah. He's in my class and he wants to talk to you."

Noah lifted his head and looked Mr Anderson in the eye. Just as he began to speak, Mrs Anderson came in to find out what was going on.

"I'm sorry," Noah began.

"You're sorry?" Mr Anderson asked. "What are you sorry for?"

"I'm sorry for painting your wall. On Monday. It was me."

Mr Anderson looked at his wife then returned his gaze to Noah. "I see." He waited to see if Noah would say anything else.

"I'm really sorry. It was wrong of me and I promise I'll never do anything like it ever again."

"I should hope not," Mrs Anderson said.

Mr Anderson scratched the side of his head. "And what do you think we should do about this? What was your name again? Was it Noah?"

"Yes sir. I could… I could clean it off."

"We've already done that," Mr Anderson said.

"I'll do anything. Anything you like. I want to make it up to you."

"How about you call in here after school each day and sweep the floor for us? Just for the next week. It's an awkward job and I sure could use a week off from it. Then we'll be even. What do you think?"

"Yes," Noah quickly agreed. "I can do that. I'll sweep the floor and I'll mop it too if you want."

"The sweeping will be enough. I can see you're a good kid underneath it all. But Noah, there's one more thing I need."

"Just name it."

"Promise me that you'll never graffiti anything ever again."

"I promise."

"Good. Now, off you go. I'll see you back here on Monday straight after school."

"Thank you. I really am sorry, Mr and Mrs Anderson."

They waved goodbye as Noah left the store.

Mr Anderson's face slowly broke into a grin. "Well," he said. "I must say a big thank you to the two of you. You told us you would find the culprit and you did it! There's no doubt about you."

Ben smiled. "It was Harrie, really. She's the one who figured it out."

"Well, I'm going to give both of you a hug."

Mrs Anderson stepped forward. "Me too. Thank you both so much."

"Any time," Harrie said. "We'll always help out if we can. You know that."

Mr Anderson stepped back and smiled. "Yes I do. Now, before you go, you must try a sample of my wife's latest creation."

Harrie grinned. She felt pretty sure this meant there was a new flavour of chocolate and she was more than happy to be one of the taste testers. Mrs Anderson walked behind the counter and picked up a container.

"I've been working on this all day and I think I've finally got it. Please try the latest variety—marshmallow delight!"

Harrie and Ben both picked up a piece of chocolate and ate it.

"Yum!" Harrie said as she chewed her mouthful. "It's so good. It tastes like rocky road. Thanks."

"No, thanks to you. To you both. Now off you go and enjoy what's left of the day."

The End

About the Author

Kristine is a lecturer of mathematics at Deakin College but enjoys writing in her spare time. Her first book, *White Space*, is a self-help book about the benefits of slowing down and improving our quality of life. She has also written the *Annie and Tia* series for children which includes three fairy stories: *The Ring of Toadstools*, *The Birthday Wish* and *The Rainbow Connection*. Her hobbies include reading, watching movies and exercising. She lives in Geelong, Victoria.

Other Books by Kristine Fitzgerald

White Space

Is your life going so fast that you can't keep up with it? Do you live according to a never-ending list of chores and deadlines? Do you feel as though life is passing you by? The world we live in today is fast, hectic and pressured. However, it does not have to be this way; you do not have to live at this pace. In White Space, Kristine Fitzgerald describes her own journey and uses clear, simple language to describe how you can regain control, live more slowly and, hence, discover the key to true happiness, peace and serenity.

The Ring of Toadstools

Annie is an eight-year-old girl who doesn't have many friends. One day, while walking by the creek, she meets a fairy named Tia. They get to know each other and a whole new world of fun, friendship, singing, games and magic opens up for Annie. But when Tia's community is thrown into danger, will Annie be able to save the day?

The Birthday Wish

Annie goes to visit her friend Tia, who is a fairy, every day after school. During these visits Annie magically turns into a fairy herself and she has a lot of fun learning how to fly and perform magic tricks. Annie joins in the excitement when a new fairy joins Tia's community. Meanwhile, at school, Annie gets to know a new girl named Sophie. Unfortunately, Sophie sits with the popular girls who are sometimes mean to Annie. Annie's birthday approaches and she has a horrible day - everything goes wrong. But when she blows out her candles and makes her birthday wish she hopes that one day Sophie will be her friend. Can Annie's birthday wish really come true?

The Rainbow Connection

Annie and her good friend Sophie love playing together, both at school and at each other's homes. One day Annie goes to watch Sophie sing in a competition. Although the day doesn't quite work out as planned, the girls grow closer and share secrets with each other. Meanwhile, in fairyland, Annie and Tia travel to the seaside, meet fairies from another community and learn to use their magic powers. One of the fairies has a tragic accident and Annie helps the group come together to deal with their loss. Annie, Tia and Sophie discover the magic that can be found at the end of a rainbow.